Zeeba
SEIZURE

Written & illustrated by
Michaela Barnes

Legal Disclaimer: this is not a medical book. If you're experiencing any of the symptoms mentioned in this book, seek medical attention.

For my two favorite girls,
Hayden and McKenzie.
I love you biggest!

Proverbs 3:(5-6)

This book is dedicated to all the brave
people battling seizures and epilepsy.
No one fights alone.

Seize the day!

Zeeba put on her favorite hot pink, sparkly skirt and unicorn headband. She was ready to start her school day.

Zeeba was heading out the door when she suddenly fell. She wasn't sure what happened. She guessed she had just tripped.

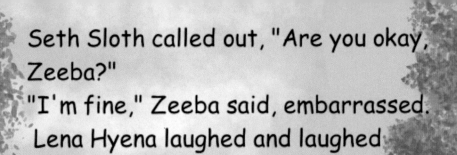

Seth Sloth called out, "Are you okay, Zeeba?"
"I'm fine," Zeeba said, embarrassed.
Lena Hyena laughed and laughed when she saw Zeeba fall.

Seth shouted, "Stop being mean, Lena!"
Lena was the meanest kid in the whole school. She laughs at everyone!

When they all arrived at school, they walked the halls and found their classrooms. Ms. Long greeted each student.

Zeeba was beginning to have a headache.

Mingo was doing her lessons on the chalkboard, while Ms. Long reviewed her answers. The other students watched and followed along. Zeeba was trying to pay attention, but she was blinking uncontrollably.

At lunch, the students were chatting and enjoying their favorite foods. However, Zeeba didn't feel like eating.

The class made their way to the playground for recess. They were all having a blast! Zeeba didn't feel like playing, but she did like spending time with her friends.

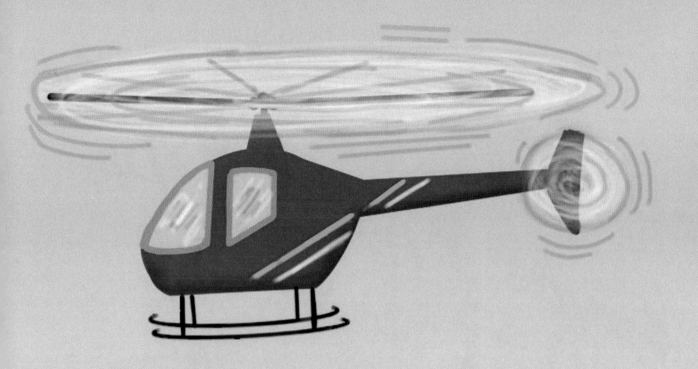

The class went inside to finish their school work. Zeeba felt strange and abruptly stopped. Her friends could tell something was wrong. "Zeeba? Zeeba? Zeeba?!" Ben Bear questioned over and over.
Zeeba just stared blankly.
"Are you alright?" Bunny asked.
After a couple of minutes, Zeeba responded.
"I don't know," she said, confused.
"I feel dizzy. It feels like there's a helicopter in my head going whoosh, whoosh, whoosh!"
Zeeba's friends were concerned about her.

All of a sudden, Zeeba collapsed backward. She was shaking and jerking! The students were frightened. Some of them ran and hid. Others covered their eyes. No one knew what to do!

Ms. Long shouted, "Go get Principal Lions!" They ran down the hall and retrieved him.

Principal Lions hurried into the classroom and called 9-1-1.An Emergency Medical Technician (EMT) came and put Zeeba on a stretcher and checked her vitals. Zeeba was scared and sobbing. She didn't want to go to the hospital alone.

"Principal Lions?" Ben asked. "Zeeba is so scared, and she shouldn't be by herself. She needs her friends. Could we go to the hospital, too? It could be like a field trip."

The whole class agreed with Ben.

After a bit of hesitation, Principal Lions agreed. He knew the students were right.
"You have to be on your best behavior. A hospital is no place to misbehave." The
class promised to obey.

They all loaded up on the school bus and followed the ambulance to the hospital.

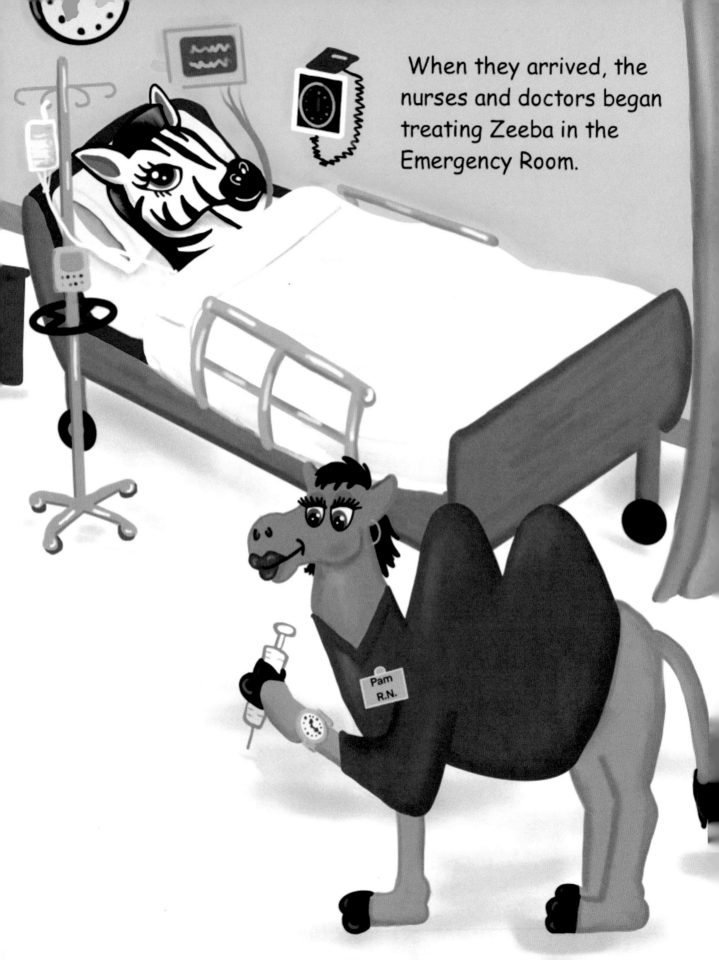

When they arrived, the nurses and doctors began treating Zeeba in the Emergency Room.

The doctors reviewed her medical history and performed a physical exam on her head and body. The doctors ordered blood and lab tests to check for other medical conditions that may cause seizures.

The nurse drew her blood and gave her medication to calm her seizures.

In the waiting room, Zeeba's friends were worried and nervous. "Is Zeeba going to be okay?" they all questioned. They prayed and sent Zeeba well wishes.

Nurse Foxy saw the sadness on their faces when she had an idea.

Maybe the staff could teach the students about seizures and ways to help Zeeba.

Principal Lions thought it was an excellent idea.

Zeeba had tests done to check her brain. Magnetic resonance imaging (MRI) and computerized tomography (CT) scans take pictures that look for physical changes in the brain.

 The lab technician performed an electroencephalogram (EEG) and put a cap on her head with wires attached. The EEG records electrical activity patterns in the brain.

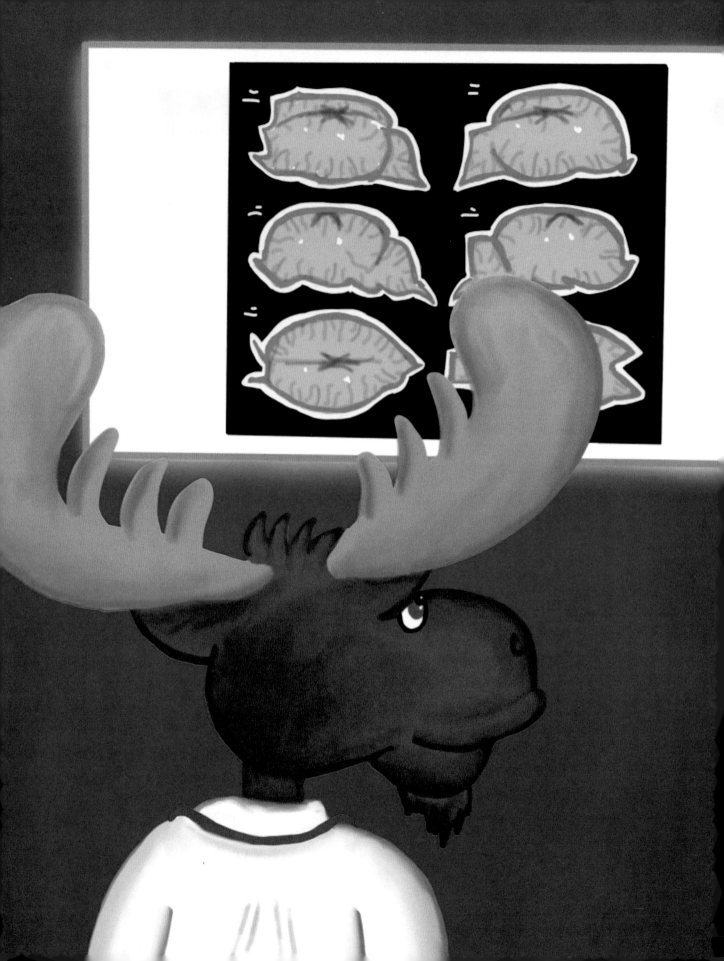

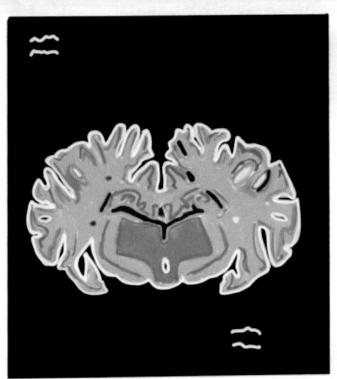

Once the tests were all done, the doctors reviewed them. They found Zeeba had some abnormal brain activity. The doctors diagnosed her with epilepsy.

When the doctor told Zeeba her diagnosis, she and her friends were puzzled. Dr. Moose decided to teach them all about epilepsy. They had many questions, and he answered them all.

"What is a seizure?" Your brain cells release tiny electrical signals to communicate with your body. These signals tell it to move, think, and do everything.A seizure occurs when cells misfire. When the electrical system of the brain doesn't operate the way it should, it creates too much electrical activity in the brain. These uncontrolled signals cause a change in awareness, movement, or sensation.

"What is epilepsy?"It is a disorder in which someone has reoccurring or multiple seizures.

"What triggers a seizure?" Flashing lights, physical or emotional stress, loud noises and music, fever, infections, lack of sleep, medication, drugs, hormonal changes in the body, and more.

"What are the types of seizures?" Generalized seizures occur when a large part of the brain produces too much electrical activity. Partial seizures only affect a small part of the brain. There are several subcategories of each. Depending on the type of seizure, varying symptoms may occur.

"What are the treatments?" Medicine, diet therapy, and surgery are options.

"How do I prevent a seizure?" Eat healthily, get plenty of rest, and avoid triggers.

"What are the signs of a seizure?" Sudden falls, lack of response for short periods, rapid blinking, confused behavior, head nodding, blank staring, lip-smacking, wandering, jerking, twitching, and shaking.

"What are the side effects of having epilepsy?" Always tired, headaches, memory loss, trouble learning, daydreaming and reoccurring thoughts are a few.

"Now, let me teach you all the first aid steps of a seizure," Dr. Moose said.

Stay and that seizure you will slay.
Gently flip them on their side and don't run and hide.
Cushion the head with something soft like a pillow from a bed.
Count 1,2,3,4..., and wait a little more.
Have no fear. Make the area safe and clear.
Remove clothing around the neck and the breathing you should check.
A lot is at stake. Support them until they're fully awake.
If the seizure lasts more than a few minutes, call 9-1-1, then you're done.

Do NOT hold down or restrain. It might cause more pain.
Do NOT put anything in their mouth, or things could go south.

"Oh, Wow! Zeeba struggles with a lot. She is brave, like a superhero. Zeeba is strong, amazing, and awesome," the class said.

Lena apologized as she cried, "I'm so sorry for laughing at you this morning. I had no idea that something was wrong, and you're having seizures. I'll never bully you or anyone ever again."

"It's okay. You didn't know." Zeeba said, calming Lena.

They gave each other a big hug.

Icee declared, "I think you're going to conquer the land of epilepsy and become queen over the seizures!"

"Well, I believe Zeeba is going to be a ninja and kick seizure-butt!" Ben exclaimed.

"You're right! I am going to defeat those seizures!" Zeeba stated confidently. The doctors and nurses helped and cheered her, too.

She was being discharged from the hospital and going home. She realized it wasn't such a scary place, after all. Her heart was so full, and she thanked them all. She was so encouraged that she had friends supporting her.

From that day forward,
Zeeba went on to seize each day!

THE END

Resources
https://www.epilepsy.com/learn/seizure-first-aid-and-safety/first-aid-seizures-stay-safe-side.htm Accessed March 2020

https://www.epilepsy.com/learn/treating-seizures-and-epilepsy.htm February 2020

https://www.cdc.gov/epilepsy/about/index.htm February 2020

Made in the USA
Las Vegas, NV
16 November 2024

11936397R00026